THIS WALKER BOOK BELONGS TO:

_____

_____

_____

First published 1988 by Hamish Hamilton Children's Books

This edition published 2013 by Walker Books Ltd
87 Vauxhall Walk, London SE11 5HJ

2 4 6 8 10 9 7 5 3 1

© 1988 Brun Ltd

The right of Anthony Browne to be identified as author/illustrator of this work has been
asserted by him in accordance with the Copyright, Designs and Patents Act 1988

This book has been typeset in New Century Schoolbook

Printed in China

British Library Cataloguing in Publication Data:
a catalogue record for this book is available from the British Library

ISBN 978-1-4063-4163-8

www.walker.co.uk

ANTHONY BROWNE

The
Little
Bear
Book

WALKER BOOKS
AND SUBSIDIARIES
LONDON · BOSTON · SYDNEY · AUCKLAND

Bear went for a walk.

"Hello, Gorilla."

"I know what you need."

"Hello, Crocodile."

"This will keep you quiet."

"Hello, Lion."

"Here's just the thing for you."

"What's this?"

"Hello, Elephant."

"This will take care of you."

"Hello, Wall."

"Bye-bye, everyone."

Anthony Browne

Anthony Browne is one of the most celebrated author–illustrators of his generation. Acclaimed Children's Laureate from 2009 to 2011 and winner of multiple awards – including the prestigious Kate Greenaway Medal and the much coveted Hans Christian Andersen Award – Anthony is renowned for his unique style. His work is loved around the world.

ISBN 978-1-4063-1327-7

ISBN 978-1-84428-559-4

ISBN 978-1-4063-1328-4

ISBN 978-1-4063-0576-0

ISBN 978-1-4063-1329-1

ISBN 978-1-4063-1930-9

ISBN 978-1-4063-1852-4

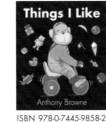

ISBN 978-0-7445-9858-2
ISBN 978-1-4063-2187-6
Board book edition

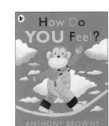

ISBN 978-1-4063-3851-5
ISBN 978-1-4063-4791-3
Board book edition

ISBN 978-0-7445-9857-5
ISBN 978-1-4063-2178-4
Board book edition

ISBN 978-1-4063-4533-9

ISBN 978-1-4063-1874-6

ISBN 978-1-4063-1873-9

ISBN 978-1-4063-1356-7

ISBN 978-1-4063-1357-4

ISBN 978-1-4063-2628-4

ISBN 978-1-4063-3131-8

ISBN 978-1-4063-1339-0

ISBN 978-1-4063-4162-1

ISBN 978-1-4063-4164-5

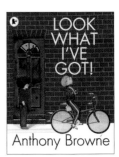

ISBN 978-1-4063-2625-3

Available from all good booksellers

www.walker.co.uk